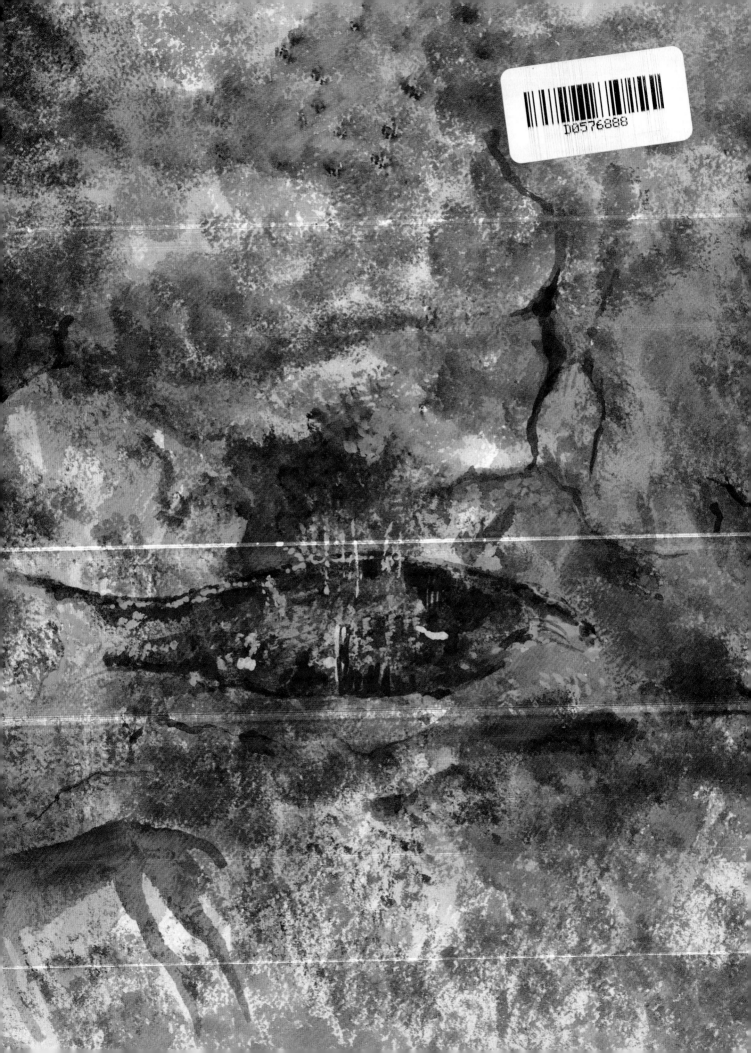

CATHERINE STOCK
Where are you going Manyoni?

Morrow Junior Books   New York

To the Bristows, especially Adam

It's Manyoni's favorite time of day. Quietly, she
slips on her dress. Her baby brother sleeps on.

Outside she splashes cold water on her face. Her mother spoons up hot porridge for breakfast.

The sky is fire-red, but a cool breeze rustles the leaves of the great gray baobab tree as Manyoni sets off down the path.

She crosses the ridge above the dry Limpopo riverbed.

Under the tall wild fig trees, a bushpig still forages
in the early morning light.

Manyoni passes the malala palms. *Ragh-gha!* bark
the baboons in fright. *Ragh-gha! Ragh-gah!*

Yimp-trrrrrrrrr… Yimp-trrrrrrrrrr! The calls of
the woodland kingfishers tremble through the air
as Manyoni crosses the fever tree pan…

and enters the shady kloof where the shy
impala feed.

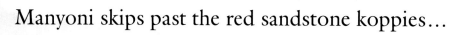
Manyoni skips past the red sandstone koppies...

and scrambles over the krantz above Tobwani Dam.

Now the sun is high and white. Manyoni's shadow dances past the mopani scrub and acacia trees…

and over the hot, dry plains.

"Matsheloni, Manyoni!" A small voice rings out
over the veld.

"Matsheloni, Tula," Manyoni greets her friend.
The two little girls hurry down the road together.

A tractor rumbles by as Manyoni and Tula reach the village. They're almost there now. The girls begin to run.

They stop at the door and smooth down their
skirts, catching their breaths.

"Good morning, Mrs. Dube," they say shyly.

Mrs. Dube glances at her watch and smiles.
"Twenty minutes," she tells them.

"Heh!" The girls clap their hands together and run
out to the school yard. They love having time to
play with their friends before class begins.

Author's Note

This story is set on the Limpopo River in Zimbabwe. Children who live in this dry, sparsely settled area, as in many other parts of rural Africa, often walk as many as two hours to school every day. I set off each morning, much like Manyoni, with my paints, paper, a bottle of water, and my constant companion, Rubbish, the dog you can see in some of these pictures.

There was nothing to fear from the wild animals in the veld. They are more afraid of humans than we are of them. But as I was quietly painting, animals would wander into the scene. I had to sketch them in quickly, before the wind changed and they caught my scent. Then they'd disappear back into the underbrush. Elephants were always a special treat. They moved silently in spite of their great size. Once when I was just about to leave the rocks above Tobwani Dam, an enormous bull suddenly appeared right below me, waded into the water, and raising his long trunk, showered himself.

The only animal that I didn't sketch from life is the leopard. I saw his spoor, or tracks, almost every morning at a spring near the camp, and once, walking home late one evening, I heard his deep, rumbling grunt.

The endpapers are copied from cave paintings made by indigenous people who lived in the area thousands of years ago. The land and its inhabitants probably appeared very much to them as it did to me.

Unfamiliar Words

The following words will be foreign to many of you, but they are included in this book to give an idea of the sound and color of the spoken word in this part of Africa.

acacia *(ah-KAY-shah)*: A flat-topped African thorn tree.

baobab *(BAY-oh-bab)*: A fat African tree with heavily folding bark.

kloof: A ravine.

krantz: A rocky cliff.

Limpopo *(lim-POE-poe)*: The large river that divides Zimbabwe from South Africa. The Limpopo only flows during the rainy season, though pools remain and animals can find water by digging into the sand.

malala palm *(mah-LAH-lah)*: A palm tree growing along the Limpopo. Elephants eat the nuts of this tree.

Manyoni *(mahn-YO-knee)*: A girl's name meaning "the birds" in Venda.

Matsheloni *(mah-cheh-LOW-knee)*: A Venda greeting meaning "Good morning."

mopani *(mo-PAH-knee)*: A hardy split-leafed African tree.

Mrs. Dube *(DOO-bay)*

pan: A temporary shallow lake.

Tobwani *(toe-BWAH-knee)*: A small tributary of the Limpopo River.

Tula *(TOO-lah)*: A girl's name meaning "quiet" in Venda.

veld *(felt)*: Grasslands or plains.

Venda *(VEN-dah)*: A language and people of northern South Africa and southern Zimbabwe.

Zimbabwe *(zim-BAB-way)*

Wildlife in this Book

In the bush, it's difficult to see animals until they move because they blend in so well with their surroundings. Some of these animals might be difficult to find.

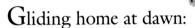

Gliding home at dawn: *a leopard*

Near the baobab tree: *a civet cat*   *a barn owl*

Flying east along the Limpopo riverbed: *knob-billed ducks*

Breakfasting on wild figs: Nearby:

vervet monkeys   *a bushpig*   *Natal francolins*

Barking at Manyoni: *baboons*

In the fever tree pan:

woodland kingfishers   *a black stork*   *a great white egret*

red-billed woodhoopoes   *white-faced ducks*   *a green-backed heron*

an African spoonbill   *black-winged stilts*

In the shady kloof:

black eagles   *impalas*   *hadedah ibises*

Inhabitants of rocky koppies: Wandering past:

At Tobwani Dam:  *a dassie*   *a gemsbok*   *an eland*

elands   *zebras*   *impalas*

kudus   *warthogs*   *wildebeests*

In the mopani scrub:

a jackal   *zebras*   *a yellow-billed hornbill*

Roaming across the plains:

elephants   *a kori bustard*   *giraffes*   *ostriches*   *kudus*

Above the road where Manyoni meets Tula:

yellow-billed hornbills

Watercolors were used for the full-color art.
The text type is 16-point Galliard.

Manufactured in China.

16 SCP 20 19 18

Library of Congress Cataloging-in-Publication Data
Stock, Catherine.
Where are you going, Manyoni? / Catherine Stock.   p.   cm.
Summary: A child living near the Limpopo River in Zimbabwe encounters
several wild animals on her way to school.
ISBN 0-688-10352-9.—ISBN 0-688-10353-7 (lib. bdg.)
[1. Animals—Fiction. 2. Zimbabwe—Fiction.] I. Title.
PZ7.S8635Wh 1993 [E]—dc20 92-29793 CIP AC